Where's Leopold? 1

Your Pajamas Are Showing!

by Michel-Yves Schmitt
illustrated by Vincent Caut

Graphic Universe™ • Minneapolis • New York

For Eliott and his mom. Thank you to Martin for his confidence from the beginning of this adventure

—Michel-Yves

A big thank-you to Michel-Yves, Martin, and to everyone who will read this book

—Vincent

Story by Michel-Yves Schmitt
Art by Vincent Caut
Translation by Carol Klio Burrell

English translation copyright © 2013 by Lerner Publishing Group, Inc.

First American edition published in 2013 by Graphic Universe™.
Published by arrangement with MEDIATOON LICENSING—France.

Où es-tu Léopold?
1/On voit ton pyjama!
© DUPUIS 2011—Caut & Schmitt
www.dupuis.com

Graphic Universe™ is a trademark of Lerner Publishing Group, Inc.

Graphic Universe™
A division of Lerner Publishing Group, Inc.
241 First Avenue North
Minneapolis, MN 55401 U.S.A.

Website address: www.lernerbooks.com

Library of Congress Cataloging-in-Publication Data

Schmitt, Michel-Yves.
    [On voit ton pyjama! English]
    Your pajamas are showing! / written by Michel–Yves Schmitt ; illustrated by Vincent Caut. — 1st American ed.
       p.   cm. — (Where's Leopold? ; #1)
    ISBN 978–1–4677–0769–5 (lib. bdg. : alk. paper)
    1. Graphic novels. [1. Graphic novels. 2. Invisibility—Fiction. 3. Brothers and sisters—Fiction.] I. Caut, Vincent, ill. II. Title.
PZ7.7.S37 2013
741.5'944—dc23   2012021660

Manufactured in the United States of America
1 – BP – 12/31/12

TA-DAAA!

Didja see?

Cool, huh?

WHAT? That's impossible! How did you do that?

I dunno!

This morning, I didn't want to go to school...

And BOOM! I turned INVISIBLE.

Except for my clothes. I can't make them disappear...

Then take off your underpants, silly!

Ugh! I don't wanna be all naked!

I did it! I just had to name all my clothes!

HA HA! Now nothing can stop Super Leopold from being totally invisible!

SPLAT!

Except...

Super Big Sister!

Hmph! I have a superpower and I can't tell anybody...

Well, yeah. That's how it is with superheroes. They have to keep it secret!

If anyone finds out your superpower, that'd be BIG DOO-DOO!

The CIA would come to the house to take you away...

We'd like a word with your son...

Did he get in trouble at school again?

They'd put you through all kinds of tests to steal your power...

He must have swallowed an eraser...

Or else they'll clone you...

You have any caramels?

Pass me a caramel, please.

Do

I'd

Hey! Caramels?

Caramels?

Who cara

And the government would send out an army of invisible Leopolds to conquer the world...

OK, show me your army...

It's right in front of you, general...

Or maybe the Mafia will kidnap you...

You can sneak all these diamonds past customs!

11

13

It's true! I trained for five years in a Shaolin monastery!

I studied martial arts, meditation, and most of all ... astral projection!

Ha ha! This girl is totally crazy!

Your heart is full of doubt, grasshopper. I shall have to demonstrate ...

Thomas is soooo cute! If only he would sit next to me at lunch!

Just ask him.

Are you out of your mind?

But why not...?

Hmph! How can I, with that pest Julie flirting all over him?

Say, Leo... would you do me a little favor...

...if I buy you caramels for a WHOLE WEEK?

22

THAT'S ENOUGH! WHAT DO YOU WANT?

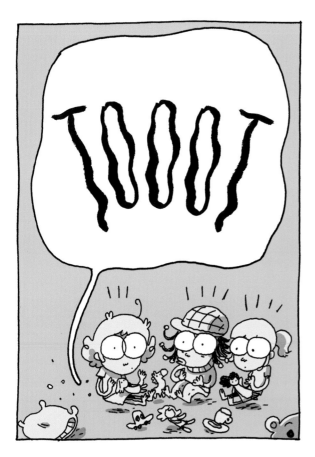

Why do I have to do it?

You're hungry, aren't you? Wake up Mom and Dad so they can make us pancakes!

Oh, all right...

You know the plan?

I go in, get the alarm clock, set the alarm to go off in five minutes...

...and I come back.

Go Go Go!

TIP TOE   TIP TOE

TIP TOE   TIP TOE

28

THE END

Readers! Can you find 12 THINGS that Leopold has sneakily moved or taken away?

Near Celine: 1) The blue T-shirt has been moved from the bed to the lamp. 2) The backpack is open. 3) One pink shoe is missing. 4) The jar of caramels is empty. 5) The red car is turned around.

In the middle: 6) The crown from the bed is on the stuffed bunny. 7) The poster has been drawn on. 8) A doll is head down in the teacup.

Near the nightstand: 9) The jar of peanut butter is empty. 10) The green book is off the stack. 11) A drawer is open. 12) The game console is gone!

Surprises!

Laughs!

Danger!

...And lots of jokes!